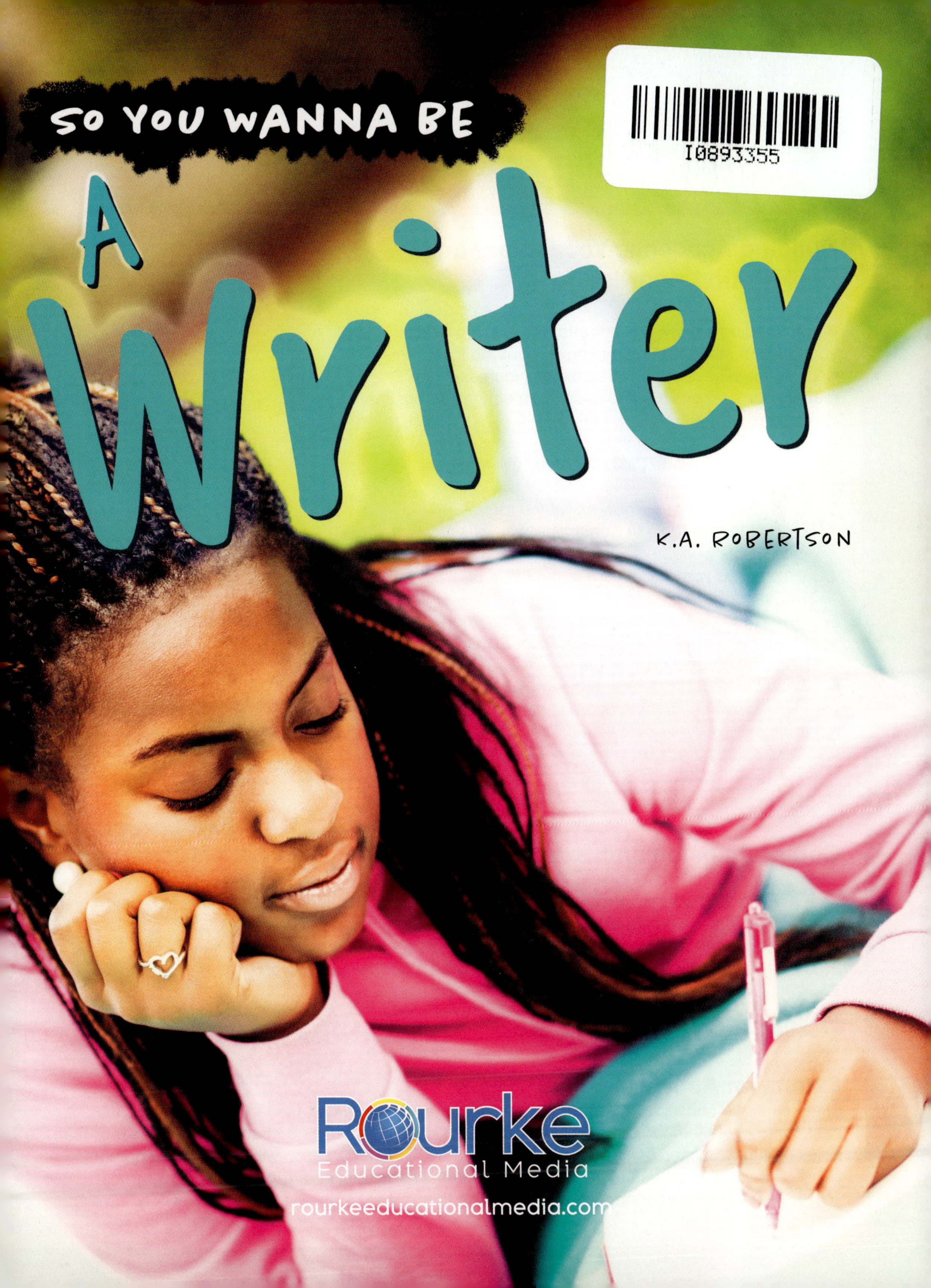

So You Wanna Be A Writer

K.A. Robertson

Rourke Educational Media
rourkeeducationalmedia.com

Before & After Reading Activities

Before Reading:

Building Academic Vocabulary and Background Knowledge

Before reading a book, it is important to tap into what your child or students already know about the topic. This will help them develop their vocabulary, increase their reading comprehension, and make connections across the curriculum.

1. *Look at the cover of the book. What will this book be about?*
2. *What do you already know about the topic?*
3. *Let's study the Table of Contents. What will you learn about in the book's chapters?*
4. *What would you like to learn about this topic? Do you think you might learn about it from this book? Why or why not?*
5. *Use a reading journal to write about your knowledge of this topic. Record what you already know about the topic and what you hope to learn about the topic.*
6. *Read the book.*
7. *In your reading journal, record what you learned about the topic and your response to the book.*
8. *After reading the book complete the activities below.*

Content Area Vocabulary

Read the list. What do these words mean?

acquire
collaborate
critique
deadlines
dialogue
fiction
freelance
intern
pitch
reputable
vet

After Reading:

Comprehension and Extension Activity

After reading the book, work on the following questions with your child or students in order to check their level of reading comprehension and content mastery.

1. *What do technical writers do? (Summarize)*
2. *Why is it important to read a lot if you want to be a good writer? (Infer)*
3. *What is the goal of copywriting? (Asking Questions)*
4. *How do your favorite books influence your writing style? (Text to Self Connection)*
5. *What specialties do content writers need to be familiar with? (Asking Questions)*

Extension Activity

Start keeping an observation notebook with you at all times. Write down interesting things you see or hear. Write about the way things make you feel, or how an experience changed your thinking. Take notes on funny or interesting conversations you have or overhear. You will soon have a notebook full of material you can use to inspire stories, shape characters, and develop plots. You can also use your notes to inspire your nonfiction writing. The things that catch your attention now can give you new ideas in the future!

Table of Contents

Write on!

Do you love to read and write? Do you browse bookstores, picturing your name on the shelves? Many professional writers did as kids. Some still do. But writing books isn't the only way to turn a passion for reading and writing into a career. There are many jobs for writers beyond the bookshelves. Some writers choose just one. Others choose to dabble in several.

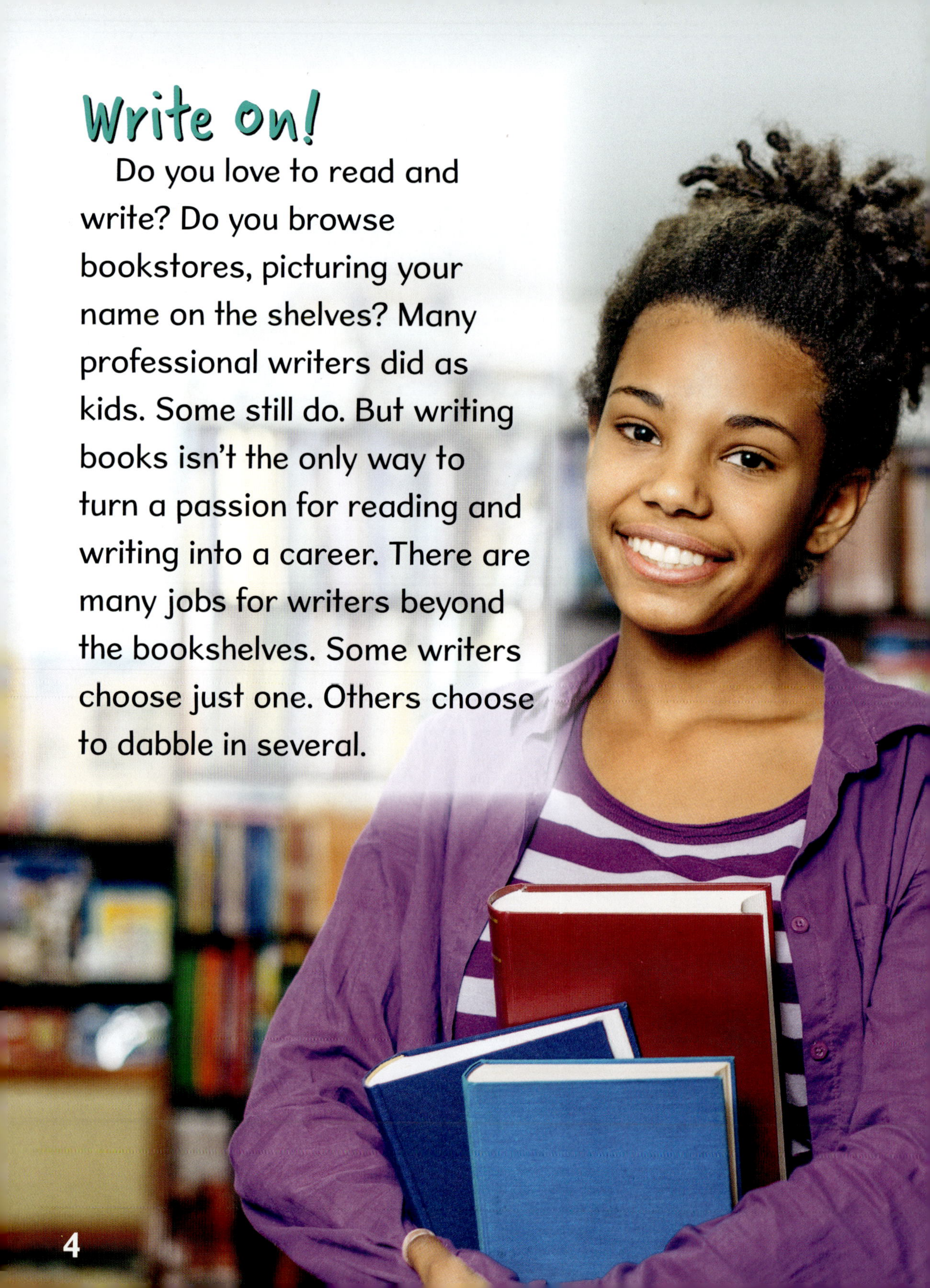

WORKING WITH WORDS

"The only kind of writing is rewriting," Ernest Hemingway said. A first draft is rarely good, much less great. Writers often go through many revisions to get to a final draft.

Newspapers, Magazines, and Blogs

Print Journalists

Print journalists write for newspapers, magazines, and news websites. They write about everything from wars to weddings. Some journalists choose a specialty, such as sports, entertainment, or politics. Some write opinion columns. Others are reporters who cover general news.

A journalist typically does research, conducts interviews, and writes articles quickly to meet **deadlines**. As each article is published, their collection of clips, or published works, grows. Their clips can help them pursue other types of writing jobs.

Ready to get started? Write for your school newspaper. Don't have one? Start one! Tools such as the free interactive printing press at www.readwritethink.org can help you create it.

PRO ADVICE

"START BY READING BOOKS, MAGAZINES, AND NEWSPAPERS. SEE HOW WORDS PAINT PICTURES. WRITE A BLOG, DIARY, SHORT STORIES, ANYTHING. FIND SOMETHING EXTRAORDINARY IN EVERYDAY LIFE AND DESCRIBE IT. NEVER LET ANYONE TELL YOU NO. A TEACHER TOLD ME I WASN'T SERIOUS ENOUGH ABOUT JOURNALISM TO BE ON MY HIGH SCHOOL PAPER. I PROVED HER WRONG." — JOE HENDERSON, JOURNALIST WITH MORE THAN 45 YEARS OF EXPERIENCE

Journalists work with editors to develop stories. An editor may assign a story, or writers may **pitch** stories for approval. To write for a newspaper or magazine, writers often need a degree in journalism or mass communication.

DID YOU KNOW?!
All reporters are journalists. But not all journalists are reporters. Reporters gather and write facts about newsworthy events. Journalists include opinion columnists and editorial writers whose writing includes analysis and opinion based on news reports.

Interns at The New York Times learn the news and business side of journalism.

GIGS FOR KIDS

Time for Kids accepts applications for student reporters every year. Check out www.timeforkids.com for information on becoming one of Time's kid journalists!

College students can **intern** at a publication for experience. Interning also introduces them to people in the business. Knowing people in the business is important! Making connections is a big part of finding writing jobs. Some writers are employed by one publication. Others **freelance** and write for several publications.

Bloggers

Anyone can start a blog. You can start writing your own blog today! Blogs are websites that are regularly updated with new content. Some blogs focus on a single topic, such as world news, community events, or cooking. Others cover several topics, much like a news website.

Writers can find paying jobs writing for popular blogs. They can also start their own blogs and earn money from advertisements. You don't always need a college degree to write for blogs. You do need to have a collection of clips to show blog editors you can write well.

FAST FACTS

Blogs make money from advertisers and sometimes product promotion. Popular blogs attract advertisers that want to reach the blog's audience.

Bloggers often rely on social media to share their stories and bring readers to their websites.

Some bloggers used to be journalists. Some bloggers were not. Journalists are trained to **vet** sources, report facts, and make it clear to readers when a story is opinion, not fact. **Reputable** publications require writers to follow these standards. Blogs do not always follow these rules. They may quote unreliable sources or report half-truths. If you want to start a blog, you should follow journalistic standards to avoid producing what's called "fake news."

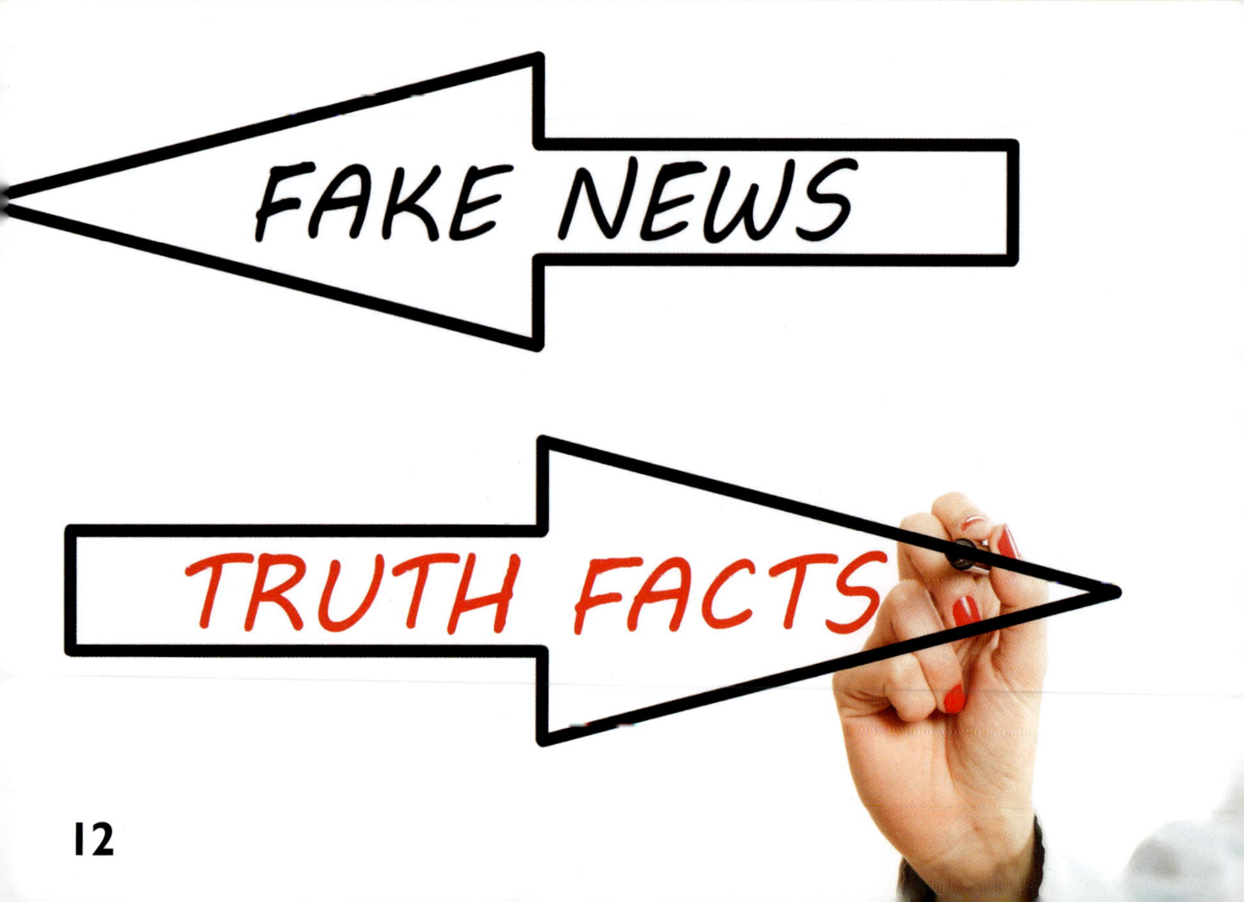

Feature Stories

Feature stories are popular in newspapers, magazines, and online. These stories can also provide inspiration for **fiction** writers' stories. Types of features include:

Human interest: A police officer buys groceries for a shoplifter. A couple skydives to celebrate their 60th wedding anniversary. A man wins a marathon after losing a leg. Human interest features tell the emotional stories of people and their concerns or achievements.

Informational: These features provide practical, social, or historical information. A story about a town's history, a how-to article on car repair, and an article about an upcoming event are examples of informational features.

Profiles: These stories are based on interviews with an individual. They give the reader insight into a person's personality, interests, and opinions or views.

Travel: Travel features tell readers about a place the writer visited and their experiences there. These include the writer's opinion about things such as hotels, entertainment, and restaurants.

Writing for Businesses and Organizations

Copywriters write text, called copy, for businesses and other organizations. The goal of their writing is to get people to take an action. Copywriters do research and conduct interviews to produce copy, often for multiple clients at once. They must write in a way that reflects the client's tone, or voice, rather than their own.

FAST FACT

Industries that employ copywriters include:

- Banks
- Insurance agencies
- Tech companies
- Manufacturers
- Government agencies
- Healthcare organizations
- Publishers
- Political organizations

Copywriters may work for a copywriting agency that serves many clients. Others may work for a single business.

Content Writers

Imagine this: You want to learn how to play the guitar. You search "How to Play Guitar" online. The first search result: Learn to Play Guitar in Three Easy Steps! You click on it and read. Then you notice the website belongs to a business that sells guitars and guitar lessons. They didn't reach you with an advertisement. You came to them because they gave you information. Content writers specialize in creating content that brings potential customers to business websites.

DID YOU KNOW?!
SEO stands for Search Engine Optimization. SEO is a collection of techniques such as keyword placement that increase traffic to a website. The goal of SEO is to make a website come up among the top results in a search engine for one or more topics.

Content writers often have degrees in English or journalism. And they aren't just good writers. Because the goal of their work is to increase web traffic, they also must be social media and SEO savvy.

Business Writers

Business writers often work as freelancers for multiple clients. Their projects may include resumes, reports, employee biographies, company newsletters, press releases, and business plans. These writers often do research and conduct interviews to create materials for their clients.

Freelance business writers are entrepreneurs. Like other freelancers, they operate as a business themselves. They use websites, social media, and networking to promote their services and get new clients.

Grant Writers

Private and public foundations award grant money for specific projects or causes. Grant writers research, write, and submit proposals for individuals or organizations applying for these grants. Some grant writers work full time for charities or nonprofit organizations. Some work as freelancers writing grant proposals for multiple clients in a variety of areas, from medical research to museums.

PRO ADVICE

"GRANT WRITING IS NOT MUCH DIFFERENT FROM THE RESEARCH PAPERS YOU WRITE FOR SCHOOL! IT'S ALL ABOUT FOLLOWING INSTRUCTIONS, PROPERLY CITING YOUR REFERENCES, AND MAKING A STRONG CASE. LEARN TO LOVE YOUR ENGLISH CLASS, AND READ AS MUCH AS YOU CAN!" —REBECCA SITTEN, PROFESSIONAL GRANT WRITER

Grant writers use their research skills to search for grants that match their clients' projects.

FAST FACT:
Grant and textbook writers often have degrees in English, creative writing, communication, marketing, or journalism. Textbook writers may also have degrees in the subjects they write about.

Textbook Writers

All kinds of schools use textbooks, from kindergarten to college! Businesses and training programs use them too. Textbook writers have great writing skills and expert knowledge in the subjects they write about.

Technical Writers

Have you ever read instructions for playing a video game or using an appliance? That's the work of a technical writer! Technical writers make complex information easier to understand. A technical writer may write about legal policies. Or they may write instructions for using a product such as computer software.

Technical writing jobs often require a bachelor's degree. Some schools offer technical writing programs.

Creative Writers

The writing careers we've touched on so far deal in facts. Ready to ditch reality? Creative writers make things up! Sometimes they get a little help from real life, though. Fiction writers are often inspired by their real-world experiences and observations. A character's traits or a fictional conversation may be based on something the writer experienced.

TV and Movies

Next time you're watching your favorite TV show or movie, note what you like about it. Is it the suspense? The funny **dialogue**? Whatever hooks you, a writer or team of writers is likely responsible for it. From comedies to dramas to late-night talk shows, writers craft much of what you see and hear.

Television writers create the plots, characters, situations, and dialogue for TV shows. Screenwriters do the same for movies.

TV writers and screenwriters don't need a specific degree. Some take television writing or screenwriting courses to develop their skills. Like other writing jobs, networking helps people make connections and find jobs.

WRITE NOW!

A search online turns up several screenwriting competitions for kids. With your teacher or parents' help, you can find reputable competitions in which to submit your work.

Want to write for TV or film? Start by being observant. Watch people interact. Take notes on funny or interesting things you see or hear. Use your experiences to create stories.

DID YOU KNOW?!

You can use a website such as www.storyboardthat.com to create a storyboard for a TV or movie script. Try coming up with your own script for the characters in your favorite TV show. Put them in a situation you haven't seen them in. What will they say and do?

PRO ADVICE

"IF YOU WANT TO BE A TV WRITER, YOU SHOULD START BY WATCHING TV. (TELL YOUR PARENTS YOU'RE DOING RESEARCH FOR YOUR FUTURE CAREER!) PAY ATTENTION TO YOUR FAVORITE SHOWS. WHAT DO YOU LIKE ABOUT THEM? WHAT KINDS OF STORIES ARE YOU MOST DRAWN TO? WHAT MAKES YOU ROOT FOR A CERTAIN CHARACTER? DISSECTING YOUR FAVORITE TV SHOWS TO FIGURE OUT WHAT MAKES THEM WORK IS A GREAT STARTING POINT FOR HONING YOUR CRAFT. YOU SHOULD ALSO READ AND WRITE AS MUCH AS POSSIBLE TO BEGIN FINDING YOUR OWN VOICE."
—JOANNA QURAISHI, PROFESSIONAL TV WRITER

Writing Books

Book authors write fiction, nonfiction, or both. They may write for kids, teens, adults, or every age. Like TV writers and screenwriters, they often use their experiences and observations in their work.

Some authors develop an idea, write a book, then submit it to publishers in hopes one will **acquire** it. Others are hired to write books based on a publisher's idea.

FAST FACT

The Writer's Market is published every year. This giant book includes information about what publishers and agents are looking for. It's a great tool for getting to know about the industry.

AGENTS

Many book publishers and production companies only work with writers represented by an agent. Getting the right agent requires research. But only after you've written the best book or script possible! Agents want to represent writers whose work they feel strongly about bringing to an audience.

Becoming a published author requires getting to know the industry and the people who work in it. Networking is important, especially for new authors. They often attend writing workshops and conferences with professional editors and agents to make contacts and get their work noticed.

Book authors don't need college degrees to be published. But they do need strong writing skills. They also need to work well with others, especially their editors. A book often goes through many rounds of edits before the publisher approves it. This process can be difficult for an author who is not open to **critique** or compromise.

DID YOU KNOW?!

Some popular book series are written by several authors writing under a single name. These ghostwriters are given a contract and outlines to follow in developing the books for the series.

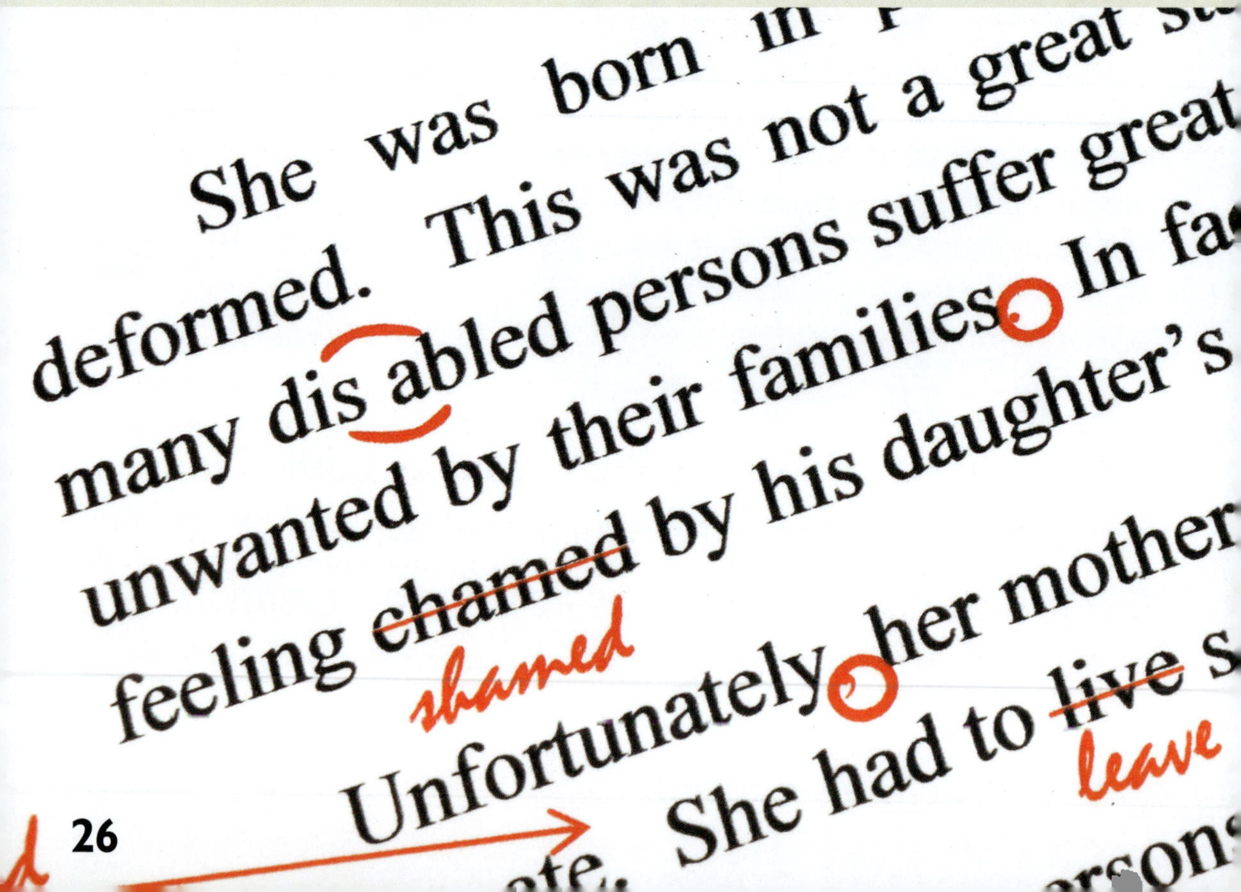

PRO ADVICE

"If you want to be a writer, you should:

1. Read adventurously and deeply. Read everything and anything that sparks your interest. And then if it's good, read it again and figure out how it works, and why it works.
2. Write every day, in the same location and time. Half an hour a day is a good amount of time to start. What you are doing is developing a writing habit. After a while, you may not be able to sleep if you haven't written. Write about anything. Experiment. Write about the everyday world. Describe people coming into rooms. Describe a flash of the eyes, the sun in the trees. Get into the habit of making art.
3. Live a life that's worth writing about. Be interesting, courageous, and passionate. If your life is all those things, then your writing will be all those things as well.
4. Don't procrastinate. Get started now! Go fast, but take your time."

—Theo Baker, author

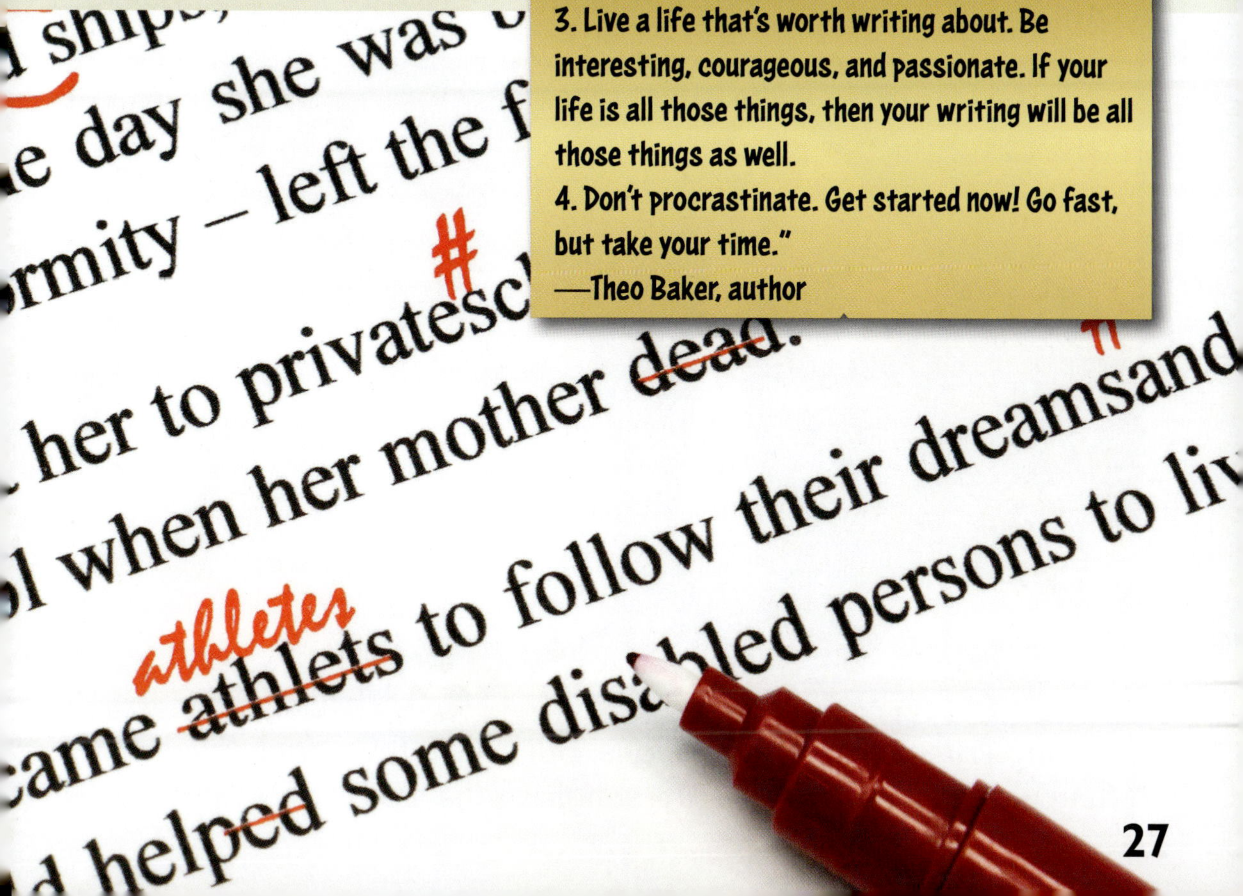

Writing Songs

What's your favorite song? What story does it tell? Songwriters write lyrics and melodies for music. Lyricists just write lyrics. These writers work with music publishers, recording artists, and record producers to create new songs. Some write alone, others **collaborate** with other writers. They may spend their days writing, attending meetings, or recording song demos.

You don't need a degree to become a songwriter or lyricist. But songwriting classes can help sharpen your skills.

Hit songwriters can make millions. But only a few reach this level. Many work day jobs and write songs on the side.

The notes you take now may become part of a book or song you write years from now.

"Most of the basic material a writer works with is acquired before the age of fifteen," acclaimed author Willa Cather once said. Observe the world and the people in it. Take notes. Read lots! Listen to music. Pay attention to the lyrics. Explore your interests. Find new interests! Learn new words. Experiment with different styles of writing. And try to write at least a little every day.

Glossary

acquire (uh-KWIRE): to get something so you own or have it

collaborate (kuh-LAB-uh-rate): work together to do something

critique (KRIT-eek): a critical analysis of a written work

deadlines (DED-lines): times when things must be finished

dialogue (DYE-uh-lawg): conversation, especially in a book, play, movie, or TV show

fiction (FIK-shuhn): stories about characters and events that are not real

freelance (FREE-lans): freelance workers get paid for individual jobs completed, and may work for various companies

intern (IN-turn): someone who is learning a skill or job by working with an expert in that field

pitch (pich): a talk or presentation meant to persuade you to do something

reputable (REP-yuh-tuh-buhl): having a good reputation; trustworthy

vet (vet): make a careful, critical examination of something

Index

Show What You Know

1. What does a copywriter do?
2. What types of college degrees are helpful for writers?
3. How can watching TV help you prepare for a writing career?
4. What is networking and why is it important?
5. What does an agent do for writers?

Further Reading

Mahoney, Ellen, *Nellie Bly and Investigative Journalism for Kids: Mighty Muckrakers from the Golden Age to Today*, Chicago Review Press, 2015.

Mazer, Anne, *Spilling Ink: A Young Writer's Handbook*, Square Fish, 2010.

Stowell, Louie, *Write Your Own Story Book*, Usborne Books, 2011.

About the Author

K.A. Robertson decided she wanted to be a writer when a story she wrote in the fourth grade was bound into a book and put in the school library. She has a bachelor's degree in English and a master's degree in mass communications. K.A. has worked as a journalist, content writer, business writer, and book author.

Meet The Author!
www.meetREMauthors.com

www.rourkeeducationalmedia.com

PHOTO CREDITS: Cover & Title Pg ©CatLane, Pg 7, 17, 23, 27 ©MariatKary, Pg 3, 14, top bar ©thawornnurak, Pg 4 Drazen Lovric, Pg 7 By Niloo, Pg 8 mizoula, Pg 9 By Ollyy, Pg 10 By Kaspars Grinvalds, Pg 11 ArtemSam, By BigTunaOnline, Pg 12 marrio31, Pg 14 pixelfit, Pg 15 LightFieldStudios, Pg 16 mediaphotos, Pg 17 By Tashatuvango, Pg 18 beaucroft, Pg 19 By RAGMA IMAGES, Pg 20 julos, krisanapong detraphiphat, Pg 21 krisanapong detraphiphat, ©fad1986, Pg 22 finwal, Pg 23 YinYang, Joanna Quarashi, Pg 24 alexskopje, Pg 25 ferrantraite, Pg 26 & 27 ©By Lamai Prasitsuwan, Pg 28 santypan, Pg 29 pepifoto,

Edited by: Keli Sipperley
Cover and Interior design by: Rhea Magaro-Wallace

Library of Congress PCN Data

A Writer / K.A. Robertson
(So You Wanna Be)
ISBN 978-1-64156-473-1 (hard cover)
ISBN 978-1-64156-599-8 (soft cover)
ISBN 978-1-64156-714-5 (e-Book)
Library of Congress Control Number: 2018930509

Rourke Educational Media
Printed in the United States of America,
North Mankato, Minnesota